My "o" Sound Box®

(This book uses only the short "o" sound in the story line. Words beginning with the long "o" sound are included at the end of the book.)

Library of Congress Cataloging-in-Publication Data
Moncure, Jane Belk.
My "o" sound box / by Jane Belk Moncure; illustrated by Colin King.
p. cm.
Summary: A little boy fills his sound box with many words beginning with the letter "o."
ISBN 1-56766-781-3
[1. Alphabet.] I. King, Colin, ill. II. Title.
PZ7.M739 Myo   2000
[E]—dc21   99-054328

My "O" Sound Box

Jane Belk Moncure

illustrated by Colin King

The Child's World

Little  had a   box.

"I will find things that begin
with my 'o' sound," he said.

"I will put them into
my sound  box."

 Little O hopped away,

hop, hop, hop.

He found otters

in a pond.

Did he put the otters into his box?

He did.

Little O found an octopus.

Did he put the octopus into the
box with the otters? He did.

But the otters did not like the octopus.

The otters hopped out of the box,

hop, hop, hop.

Little  put a top on the box so the octopus could not get out.

Then he put the otters on top
of the box.

Away he went, hop, hop, hop.

Then Little  found an

ostrich.

He hopped on the ostrich.

"Hop," he said.

But the ostrich would not hop.

So Little  put the ostrich on top of the box.

Now the box was heavy.

Little  found an

OX.

"You are just what I need for my box," he said.

Away they went,
  hop,
    hop,
      hop . . .

all the way home.

Little  took his things out of the box.

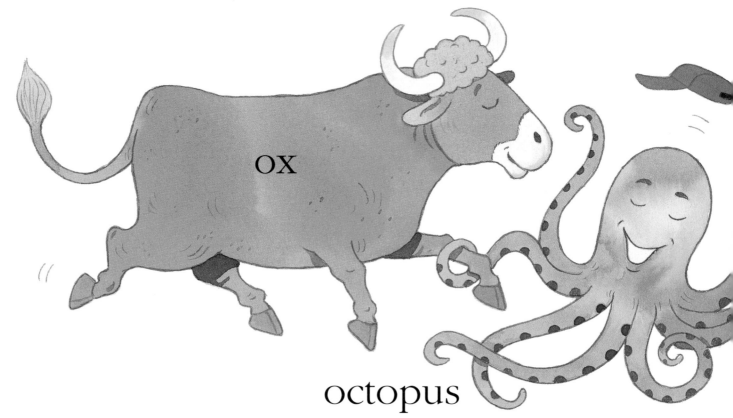

ox

octopus

ostrich

What funny things he had!

otters

Can you read these words  with Little O ?

October

S	M	T	W	T	F	S
1	2	3	4	5	6	7
8	9	10	11	12	13	14
15	16	17	18	19	20	21
22	23	24	25	26	27	28
29	30	31				

olives

ocelot

operator

oranges

Little  has another sound in some words. He says his name, "o."

Can you read these  words? Listen for Little 's name.

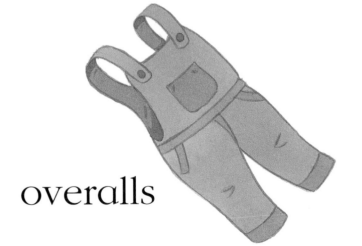

overalls

okra

oatmeal

opal

ocean

ABOUT THE AUTHOR AND ILLUSTRATOR

Jane Belk Moncure began her writing career when she was in kindergarten. She has never stopped writing. Many of her children's stories and poems have been published, to the delight of young readers, including her son Jim, whose childhood experiences found their way into many of her books.

Mrs. Moncure's writing is based upon an active career in early childhood education. A recipient of an M.A. degree from Columbia University, Mrs. Moncure has taught and directed nursery, kindergarten, and primary grade programs in California, New York, Virginia, and North Carolina. As a former member of the faculties of Virginia Commonwealth University and the University of Richmond, she taught prospective teachers in early childhood education.

Mrs. Moncure has travelled extensively abroad, studying early childhood programs in the United Kingdom, The Netherlands, and Switzerland. She was the first president of the Virginia Association for Early Childhood Education and received its award for outstanding service to young children.

A resident of North Carolina, Mrs. Moncure is currently a full-time writer and educational consultant. She is married to Dr. James A. Moncure, former vice president of Elon College.

Colin King studied at the Royal College of Art, London. He started his freelance career as an illustrator, working for magazines and advertising agencies.

He began drawing pictures for children's books in 1976 and has illustrated over sixty titles to date.

Included in a wide variety of subjects are a best-selling children's encyclopedia and books about spies and detectives.

His books have been translated into several languages, including Japanese and Hebrew. He has four grown-up children and lives in Suffolk, England, with his wife, three dogs, and a cat.